WHERE THE HEART GOES

WHERE

THE

HEART GOES

~A Western Novella~

SHIRLEY SORBELLO

First paperback edition November 2021

ISBN 978-1-7377026-0-3 (paperback)
ISBN 978-1-7377026-1-0 (e-book)

www.shirleysorbello.com

PREFACE

"Where the Heart Goes" is narrated by Rebecca Adams, a strong, unforgettable woman who travels from Pennsylvania to Texas to follow her dreams in the mid-1800s. She shares with the reader clips of the most memorable and poignant moments of her life, beginning in young adulthood. It's an ordinary life in many ways, woven with themes of love, romance, motherhood, abuse, spirituality, and death. Yet, Rebecca has a remarkable ability to learn and reflect from the experiences of her heart. She aptly sums it up with, "It's strange how the heart can take the reins from you but still allows you to think you're in control."

When I published two short stories several years ago about Rebecca's life, I had no idea her saga was not yet complete—on paper, that is. The original idea was inspired from an unusual daydream I had of a man riding a bronco, who became the character John Coulter. From there, the story took on a life of its own and developed into "That's Just the Way It Is" and "Return to Texas."

During the last year, this follow-up novella has begged to be written. It's a deeper and much expanded version of the earlier short stories. Perhaps its basic theme—deep love that lives in the heart and soul never truly dies—bears repeating in a world that often appears loveless. It has been a joy and a heart-warming experience to write this piece. I hope you will find it the same to read.

Many thanks to my family and the many friends who have supported and encouraged me along the way.

CHAPTER 1

Flashes of memories from that lifetime creep into my consciousness. I'm staring at a weathered barn through a kitchen window. Calico curtains blow in the dusty wind, dancing to the familiar hum of cows mooing in the distance. Warm air whips across my face, entering the house as a welcomed visitor on a hot, Texas day in 1875. I'm Becky, married with four children, to a man I both love and hate.

***

"Becky, Becky, get yourself out here," John shouted from the corral. "This heifer's gettin' ready to birth."

I flew out the back door and glimpsed our youngest, Matthew, crouched over by the side of the barn. He was whimpering softly as tears streamed down his cheeks.

I knelt in front of him. "Matty, what's wrong?"

"Ow!" he cried out when I began to hug him. "Mama, I'm okay."

"Let me see." I pulled up his shirt and winced at the bright red belt marks across his back.

"Oh God, not again. Go inside, Matty. Tell Emily to put some salve on your back and stay in the house today."

"But Pa wants me to—"

"It's gonna have to wait. Now go inside. Do what I say."

I stormed into the barn as John barked, "Calf's comin' out, just needs a little more help."

"The calf will have to wait," I said with my hand on my hip. "I wanna know why you beat Matty this time."

"That boy's so darn careless. He spilled nails all over the hay where the stock can get at 'em," John said with a frown. "Besides, a good beatin' will make a man outta him."

"He's only five years old!"

"Hell, I was gettin' whipped two or three times a week when I was his age," John shouted.

"Johnny, that doesn't make it right. It's gotta stop. Do you hear me?"

"I have to do what I think best. Boys need to be strong. Now get on with helpin' the cow!"

I felt each slap of the belt that John gave the boys deeply inside of me. It went to that place where a mother's sorrows gather when bad things happen to her children—things she can do nothing about.

John often said he didn't believe in hitting women, so I guess that's why Emily and I escaped the physical expression of his wrath for many years. One time he told me his drunken father had shoved his mother when she confronted him about his infidelity. With no emotion, John described his parents' fight and how she'd fallen and hit her head against their cast iron wood stove. I cried when he told me he'd watched his mother die that day. He was barely ten years old.

Many times, I noticed John staring into space. His face, void of emotion, appeared frozen by a fleeting childhood memory. He rarely shared his thoughts, but he didn't have to. I could tell by his startled cries in the middle of the night that many of those experiences had shattered his spirit early in life.

CHAPTER 2

John's upbringing was in stark contrast to my own. I was born in Philadelphia to kind, loving parents and lived with them until I was twenty-five. I remember the day I first breeched the subject of moving west.

"What's that you're drawing, Rebecca?" my father, Daniel Adams, asked. I glanced back over my shoulder and noticed his blue eyes squinting as he peered at my artwork.

"It's a cowboy. Sort of like the one I dream about."

"Really? You still dream of cowboys?"

"Yes, Papa, from time to time."

"But you're a grown woman now."

"I realize that, but sometimes I wonder if I'm meant to be a mail-order bride because—"

"Oh, Rebecca, banish that thought! You'll have a great career as a design artist and businesswoman here."

"What in the world are you two talking about?" my mother, Jane, said as she walked into our parlor. She flashed her pretty smile.

"Mother, do you think I should move to the West and marry a handsome, young cowboy?"

Mother stared through her wired spectacles at my drawing. "Perhaps," she replied slowly. My father's mouth flew open.

***

I'd been dreaming of living in the West for a while. Popular journalists fueled my interest by their glamorous portrayal of western life. I'd even answered two newspaper ads from men in Texas looking for wives. I wondered, though, how a city-bred lady would fare in that culture. It certainly appeared challenging, and I came to realize that a woman required the support of a devoted husband and family to survive the harsh life there. Although I fancied myself as a gutsy, strong woman, I was afraid of going to Texas alone. Nevertheless, fantasies of marrying a Texan invaded my thoughts almost daily.

My father had paid a lot of money to send me to fine schools—both the Young Ladies Academy of Philadelphia and the Philadelphia School of Design for Women—to provide opportunities for me aside from being a wife. At the very least, he hoped that one day I'd continue to run and even expand the family dry goods store into something bigger and better. While I appreciated these educational opportunities and his vision for my future, it wasn't mine. I knew

I was intelligent and artistic and believed these skills would make me an excellent homemaker and mother. I welcomed the opportunity to have a family of several children.

***

Two years later, my life changed forever. The textile industry had exploded, and Papa's shop was profiting from the influx of people moving into the area to work in the mills.

"The shop's making more money now than I ever thought possible, and I can trust Robert to manage everything," Papa said to Mother and me one night. "I'm considering expanding the business into another area of the country. Becky, where was it you wanted to live?"

This time, it was my mouth that flew open. I'd recently found a job in a small, fashionable shop on Chestnut Street where I designed dresses. In addition, a young store owner I had met in town was courting me. My future was falling into place here.

My heart beat faster as I heard myself saying, "Texas, somewhere in Texas."

"Your mother and I've been talking. We decided that, apparently, we share the same spirit of adventure as you."

I glanced at Mother, who had a big smile on her face. "Really?"

Papa laughed. "Rebecca, if your eyes get any bigger, they surely will pop out of their sockets. But yes, if you're sure you want to move there, I'll see what I can work out."

"Oh, my goodness, Papa, yes. I'm sure," I said as I threw my arms around his neck. I was crying joyful tears that I didn't fully understand. However, the peace in my heart reassured me that this was a comfortable decision for the direction my life should take.

***

Chaos abounded for the next six months. My parents decided to rent out their home and determined that Papa's store manager would hire an assistant and continue to run the shop. My father established some contacts in Dallas and had even rented a small, commercial storefront on the outskirts of town before we left. We would have to find a place to live once we got there. Worst of all was the decision of what to take with us!

For the past few months, I had been exchanging letters with a young banker who lived in Dallas. Although I hadn't discussed it with my parents, I was sure that Mother knew about him because she often picked up the mail. I took the fact that we were moving to Dallas as a sign that he might be the one I was looking for even though he was not a cowboy.

***

On a rainy day in May 1859, we boarded the train to western Pennsylvania. I had never traveled farther than twenty miles west of Philadelphia, so for me it was an exciting opportunity to see the grand mountains of Pennsylvania as well as the many thick, lush forests and beautiful streams along the way. After we reached Pittsburgh, short stretches of railway lines alternated with long stage drives all the way to Dallas.

I adored the small homesteads and farming communities that popped into view along the rolling, green landscape from time to time. Bustling cities like St. Louis and New Orleans were in sharp contrast to the vast number of sleepy towns with only a couple of stores and a town hall.

Fortunately, there were only a few mishaps. A wheel on the stage broke in Indiana, and the coach rolled over into the middle of a cornfield. Luckily, no one was hurt. Then there were those few hours when a waystation was closed in Tennessee. We became so hungry and parched that heated exchanges over the sanity of our decision to travel to Texas developed.

However, they quickly abated once we had a good meal. Later, Mother got sick a few times from the heat in the South as we traveled into Louisiana. But overall, my parents survived almost as well as I did. I wish I could say the same for our luggage.

After three weeks of smelly stagecoaches and dusty, sooty railway cars, we arrived in Dallas. I'll never forget the horrid color of the tub water after my first bath there! There was no doubt the trip had been exhausting, uncomfortable, frustrating, and much too long, but it was also exciting beyond my wildest dreams.

The area around Dallas intrigued me because it was so wide open, a far cry from the overcrowded streets of Philadelphia. Pretty rivers and patches of thick forests dotted the nearby countryside. To the west, it was grassy, but drier and flat as if someone had ironed it. I could even watch the sun set after a short walk to the edge of town. It took us two months to get settled in this unfamiliar land. By then, I still felt out of place, but enthusiastic about the new challenges and adventures each day brought forth.

***

You're probably wondering if I met the banker. I contacted him once we arrived in Dallas, and he came to the hotel where we were staying. Josh was a thin, blond-haired man who made a great first impression by helping us to find a small house to rent. Papa liked that he was a banker who could connect him with other businessmen in the area. He even took out a small loan from the bank Josh managed. On the other hand, Mother did not take to him as easily and told me to be cautious.

After four months of courting, Josh proposed. I was growing fond of him, and we enjoyed good times together. I should have been happier, but it didn't feel right. Isn't this what I had wanted? Well, not quite.

"Rebecca, will you do me the honor of becoming my wife? I've loved you from the day I saw you. We'll have a fine life together. Many children, if you wish."

"Let me th-think about it, Josh." I stumbled over the words as he flashed a lovely, white gold filigree ring laced with several small diamonds.

"It was my mother's wedding ring. I'd be honored if you would wear it as my wife."

A month later, I met a real cowboy.

CHAPTER 3

I remember the first day I saw John Coulter. He was a tall, lanky man with black curls who came strolling into my father's general store looking for some navy thread to sew his pants. His charming smile and sparkling, dark eyes left me somewhat mesmerized.

"Is your wife going to fix them for you?" Those words flew out of my mouth.

"No, miss. I don't have a wife. I sew my own pants."

He grinned as I felt my face turning red. John began courting me after his second trip to the store a few days later. He appeared a kind, intelligent man with an underlying strength that I found appealing. I laughed often at his antics, and when he thought I looked too serious, he would tease or kiss me to make me smile. I felt happy and contented when we were together.

Three weeks after John and I began keeping company, Josh asked me to go riding. It was a pleasant summer morning, and soon we stopped near a shaded creek about three miles from town to rest and cool off. We sat on the ground and shared water from Josh's canteen.

"You ride well, Becky," Josh said.

"I know," I said with a grin. "When I was twelve, Papa bought me a pony, and I loved to sprint through the backstreets of Philadelphia. I still miss Buttercup. She was my best friend for the longest time."

Josh began stroking my hair and kissing me as he cupped my face in his hands. The taste of liquor in his kiss surprised me.

"Josh, have you been drinking?"

"No, of course not. It's barely noon."

"I thought I smelled liquor."

"You're mistaken, Rebecca. Besides, you're not my wife so you can't tell me what to do."

I glared at him. "I told you I'd think about it. Let's ride back now."

"You know, you're missing out on a good opportunity with me. After all, you're just a girl who answers mail-order bride ads and then teases men with other guys."

"That's not true. I can't marry someone I don't love!"

"I'll make you love me," he said as he grabbed my shoulders and shoved me down onto the ground. He pushed his body against me and began sliding one hand up my thigh as he fondled my breasts with the other.

When I resisted, he held me even tighter and began tearing off my blouse. "Let go of me, you fool!"

By now he was lying completely on top of me, but before he could do the unthinkable, I poked him in the eyes, shoved his chin back, and managed to kick him in the groin. After pushing him off me, I ran to my horse and rode home as fast as I could. My parents forbade him to return to our house when he showed up two hours later.

John and I started seeing each other more often now that Josh was out of the picture. He began to fit perfectly into my dream of living on the western frontier with a cowboy. Seven months later, we married.

***

That day arrived I had dreamt of since childhood. Mother helped me into my white, satin and lace gown.

"Becky, this dress is exquisite. The style is so unique."

"It looks just the way I wanted it to."

"You have so much talent. I hope it doesn't go to waste out here."

"Don't worry, Mother. I will use it as best I can. I know this isn't the life you wanted for me, but I am confident I'll be happy here with John. I hope you will come to see that."

Mother opened her mouth to say something and stopped. Tears welled up in her eyes, and she held me for the longest time. This surprised me because she generally said what came into her mind and was not an affectionate person.

We married that day on Edgar Coulter's cattle ranch, about five miles west of Dallas, near a small stream under a tiny cluster of cedar elm trees. I remember the warmth of the sunlight on my face as I walked from the house on my proud father's arm to stand among our parents and friends. When I looked into John's loving eyes and said my vows, it seemed as though we were seeing clear into each other's souls.

John and his younger brother, Chester, along with some ranch hands, had begun building a log cabin on the edge of their father, Edgar's, property not too long after John and I had met. John later told me he had an inkling that things would become serious between us and had asked his father to deed off a section of his land. By the time the wedding came along, my parents and John's father had purchased all the furniture and supplies needed to start out life together in this quaint, five-room house. It was fortunate for us that Papa owned a store where he could order most of our necessities even if it took a while for them to come in. The rooms were a great deal smaller than I was used to, but I sure loved that big, front porch for sitting out after a busy day. My body ached constantly for the first six months as I slowly became aware of the painful differences between living in Texas as a wife on the edge of the prairie and in Philadelphia as a daughter in my parents' posh, city home. Despite the long arduous days, there grew a peacefulness in my heart that I had never experienced before. It was as if I'd finally come home.

***

Two years after we arrived in Texas, my parents sold the store and moved back East. A series of events had led up to this decision. Papa came to realize that I couldn't run the store with my responsibilities in caring for a family. Then, a fire in July singed the store and destroyed some of his supplies, while dissention continued to permeate Dallas over the issue of slavery. Mother, who still hadn't adjusted to western life, became extremely upset when Texas succeeded from the Union. That did it! Papa thought it best they return to Philadelphia, not only for Mother's sake, but also because he believed a war would create a scarcity of both stock and customers.

Two months before they left, Emily had been born on a chilly, February day. John stayed with me the whole time while Chester rounded up my parents and the nearest doctor. This adorable, little girl's arrival over-joyed us all. I wondered if it disappointed John a bit that she was not a boy, but he never said so then. This was the second happiest day of my life. You must realize by now, the first one was the day I married John.

It was such a thrill to see my parents play with their only grandchild, but now it became an even more painful loss for them to leave both of us in Texas. They departed in April 1861 on the day the Civil War began. The memories of that tearful goodbye stayed with me for too many years.

CHAPTER 4

John and his family made a great deal of money prior to the war. Edgar Coulter had negotiated government contracts to provide beef to the frontier forts and Indian reservations in western Texas. Sometimes, they even drove cattle to the Rocky Mountains in areas where the gold prospectors lived.

Around the time of our marriage, certain states became reluctant to buy Texas cattle because of the Texas fever epidemic. When the Civil War began, John found a willing buyer in Oklahoma. Few men were available to work the cattle ranches, so the demand became more difficult for John and his father to manage. Chester had been forced to enlist, but there was no doubt Edgar greased someone's palm to keep John and him home. I didn't ask questions, just remained grateful that John was not away risking his life. Our cows, chickens, and family vegetable garden provided us with plenty to eat.

We survived the four long years of war better than many of our friends and neighbors. Some men never returned, and others that did found their family had either moved away or was living day to day, hungry and desperate. We helped others with food as best we could. Although John was away from home more frequently driving small herds of cattle, I was reassured by the fact that John's father lived only half a mile away in case I needed help.

***

The early years of my life with John were happy ones, splattered with incredibly romantic moments. He brought out a fierce passion in me I had never known existed before we married. Shortly after our fifth wedding anniversary, John and I dropped four-year-old Emily off at a neighbor's home, so we could spend time alone and enjoy a romantic ride under a star-studded sky. We stopped by at a tavern near Fort Worth that had reopened since the war ended. After a bit of steak washed down with a little whiskey punch, we rode home wrapped in each other's arms. As John sang some of his favorite songs to me, I remember looking up at the magnificent sky. It was just before the moon rose, and the stars sparkled so brightly—just like tiny diamonds tossed upon a piece of indigo velvet.

John suddenly stopped the horses and said, "I can't wait. Let's go in the back."

I giggled. "Right here? I hope we don't spook the horses."

"Wouldn't that be an adventure! Don't worry, Bec. I'll take it easy." John chuckled while he pulled the wagon off to the side of the road behind a small clump of oak trees.

I let down my long, auburn hair, tossed my blue dress to the side and stretched out on the woolen blanket that John had put down for us. I shivered until he climbed on top, covering me with his firm, warm body and an abundance of gentle kisses. After our lovemaking, we snuggled together under the blanket, basking in the romantic glow of the strawberry moon.

"Becky, I love you so much. Please, never leave me. I wouldn't know what to do without you."

"John, what makes you think I'd leave?" I replied, somewhat surprised. "I love you."

"You're all educated. You could've done better than me." He hesitated. "You're a damn good-lookin' woman too. Any guy in town would've been thrilled to have you as a wife."

"I didn't want just any guy."

"I worry I'll come home from a drive and find you took Em back to Philadelphia. Your parents couldn't stick it out. It's dang tough for a woman out here."

"It doesn't matter. My life's here. You remember how my father wanted me to marry Josh Parker because he had some money and wore a suit?"

"I can hardly forget that. For a while, I thought he'd win out."

"Papa thought my life would be easier with Josh because of the money and lifestyle. But that didn't matter to me. I wanted to marry the man I loved. You know what a romantic fool I am."

"Sure do." John grinned and kissed the tip of my nose.

We lay there wrapped in each other's arms while we watched the pale moon slowly make its journey high into the sky. I felt so close to John that night and always believed that Owen was a joyful result of our passionate ride home. It surprised me he had expressed his fear of losing me because John rarely displayed any vulnerability.

***

John was thrilled when Owen was born and even more so when Josiah came along the following year. "Bec, do you know how much this means to us? In five or six years, these boys will be ready to help out here and earn some of their keep."

I glared at him while thoughts flew through my mind. I believed that a child was a gift from God, to be treasured for all the love and special qualities they brought to their lives, as well as that of their loved ones. I also reckoned I'd better teach them to read and write early on as I suddenly realized how the education I wished for them to have was already in serious jeopardy.

John must have thought better of his words, and a few minutes later remarked, "You know I love all our children. It's just that the boys can help more on the ranch and even carry on the business after we're gone."

"I realize that male children are valued by men more than little girls. It seems truer here than in the East."

John leaned over and kissed me on the forehead. "I really do love you and Em with all my heart. Don't ever forget that."

Matty was born four years later. Need I say more?

***

Despite some differences in values, John and I shared many joyful, family moments over the years with our young children, sitting around on winter nights in front of a blazing fire, singing and listening to John play his guitar.

"Pa, will you play 'Buffalo Gals?'" Emily loved that song and would sing with John, "and dance to the light of the moon," at the end of each stanza.

"Pappy, play 'Skip to my Lou,' pleeease," Owen usually chimed in after John finished "Buffalo Gals." He and Josiah loved to run around in a circle while they decorated the song with their laughter. Matty often lay in his cradle nearby gurgling contentedly. John would smile as he watched his children enjoying his music. He used to say that music flushed out his worries when he was troubled. It was the picture-perfect scene of a loving family.

For a while, these sweet memories helped to get us through some later bumpy times. John became moodier as the years passed, especially after he took up drinking as a hobby. He lost interest in music and rarely touched his guitar. As his responsibilities grew with the family cattle business, he became increasingly negative. This was especially evident after his father died. He and Chester began fighting over the estate. It was that year John totally forgot our thirteenth anniversary. Even though I realized worry consumed him over settling the estate and a recent surge of cattle rustling, it bruised my feelings. He didn't apologize when I later mentioned it, and I began to feel that he no longer cared about me.

Chapter 5

As time went on, John seemed to trust no one, not even me. In fact, after fifteen years of marriage, he became very jealous. It was also around this time he began hitting Matty more often.

Jake Johnson knocked at our back door one night. "Mrs. Coulter?"

"Hi, Jake, come on in and sit down. Would you like some coffee?"

"Don't mind if I do. I have somethin' I wanna ask you. My Mary's thirteen, and I reckon she needs to be around a woman more—a young woman like you, not like her grandma. Her ways are too old-fashioned, and Mary's startin' to sass her a bit. You have a daughter about her age, don't ya?"

"Yes, our Emily's fourteen."

"Well, I was wonderin' if I could drop off Mary once in a while to spend time with your girl and you. I don't think she'd be no bother. She could help Emily do her chores."

"Yes, that would be fine, Jake. And call me Becky, please."

"Thank you, ma'am," he said with a smile. "The coffee's good. Mine tastes like dishwater half the time."

"It must be hard without your wife," I said. Jake had lost his wife in childbirth with their second son.

"Damn hard. She's gone five years now, and it seems like forever." He pulled out a handkerchief to wipe his eyes.

I put my hand on Jake's arm to comfort him. At the same moment, John suddenly opened the back door.

"What's goin' on? What the hell are you doin' here?" he said to Jake with a scowl on his face.

"Talkin' to your missus about my Mary. I was wondering if she could help me a bit."

"We don't run a babysittin' service."

"I ain't askin' for that. I just wanted Mary to spend a little time with your wife and daughter."

"Huh, we'll see," John said with a scowl. "Shouldn't you be gettin' back to your children? Next time talk to me, not my wife. I don't allow no farmhands in the house."

"Jake, you're our neighbor too. Please excuse my husband's rudeness."

"I'd better be goin'."

"Drop off Mary one day next week, Jake. It'll be okay, won't it, John?"

"I reckon," he said, glaring at me, his breath reeking of whiskey. "But don't make it a dern habit."

"No, sir. Good evenin' to ya." He tipped his hat to me. "Ma'am."

"What the devil's wrong with you? Carryin' on with a scalawag like that? Good thing I came in when I did.

In a couple more minutes he'd of had you bare-assed on the table."

"For heaven's sake, John. What's the matter? Calm down. The children will hear you."

"I'm not the problem. And don't you ever go against what I say in front of the cowboys, or anybody, for that matter." John was getting red in the face, and his lips were protruding. I thought for a moment he might spit on me. I stood up as he suddenly raised his arm and slapped my face with the back of his hand. He followed up with a more painful blow on the other cheek.

"I won't have you carryin' on with him. I'm firin' him tomorrow!"

"John," I cried. "Don't you dare fire him. That man has children depending on him. There's nothing going on between me and Mr. Johnson. Please come to your senses!"

Emily and the boys had run into the kitchen by now. Four pairs of eyes, wide open with fear, stared in silence. Emily soon rushed over and put her arms around my waist.

"Get away from her, Em. I'm not through yet," he yelled as he took off his belt.

I nodded to Emily, and she stepped back. "Take your brothers into the parlor," I told her.

John grabbed me by the arm. I struggled when he began hitting me with the buckle end, leaving deep gashes in the skin on my neck and arms. I tried to cover my face, and my hands became streaked with blood. After I started screaming, Emily came running and tried to pull his arm back. John pushed her away, and I heard her cry out as she banged her head against the wall.

"Stop it! Let me go! I'm pregnant."

He froze and glared at me. "Who's the father?"

"It's you! I swear on my grandmother's grave—it's you," I said, while I tried to catch my breath. "What in God's name has gotten into you?"

That's the last thing I remember until I opened my eyes a while later. I was lying on a couch in the parlor, and Emily was sitting alongside of me, holding one of my bandaged hands. When I looked up at her, I noticed her eyes were red and swollen.

"Mama, Pa went to fetch the doctor. You passed out and started bleeding all over the floor."

I could feel the tears running down my cheeks. "I must have lost your baby sister. I'm so sure it was a girl." Pain shot through me as I attempted to move into a more comfortable position.

"I put salve on the cuts, and I bandaged your hands."

"Is your head okay?"

"Yes, I had a headache but it's going away."

"I'm glad. Where are the boys?"

"Pa took Matty with him. Josiah and Owen are out doing their chores." Emily hesitated. "Mama, why did Pa beat you?"

"Your father thinks I dishonored him with Mr. Johnson."

"But you didn't, did you?"

I shook my head and mumbled, "No."

"It wasn't right for him to beat you." She sighed. "I hate him for that. I'll never marry a man who would beat me."

"It's not right to hate your father. You must respect him," I said, feeling somewhat hypocritical. I quickly thought of something else so I wouldn't start crying again.

"Ma, close your eyes and rest," Emily said as she kissed me on the forehead. "I'll stay with you 'til the doctor comes."

A day later, John apologized to me and the children, but things were never the same between us. My youthful fantasies continued to be crushed by a reality I could never have imagined when we first married. The devotion to my family remained, but the door to my heart had slammed shut. Never again would I open it to him, nor would I allow him to abuse me physically like that. My belief that love could make anything work had died. Years of watching John hurt our children had nurtured a hatred growing deeply inside of me. My love for him was slipping away, and I found it harder and harder to believe he still loved me, even though he occasionally said so. For whatever reason, John never hit me again.

Chapter 6

John whipped Owen and Josiah less often when they reached their teenage years. The boys had grown quickly and were almost as tall as their father. Quick to defend themselves, they had matured rapidly, both physically and mentally. Despite all the abuse, they seemed intelligent, sensible young men that I was very proud of. I wondered if John had become afraid that they might gang up on him.

I worried more about Matty, who often appeared sullen and withdrawn. Some nights he would cry out in his sleep. His brothers would calm him down and let him sleep in their bed when he was scared. More than once, Owen took the blame for something Matty had done to spare him the pain of John's belt. I felt confident they would help him when I wasn't nearby.

One day, Matty came into the kitchen with blood on his hands. "Ma, I can't do everything my brothers can. Is that why Pa hates me so much?"

Everything in me wanted to go find John, rip off his belt and thrash him senseless with it. Somehow, I managed to stay calm. "Oh, Matty, no. Pa doesn't hate you. Deep inside he loves you very much."

"It sure doesn't seem so," he cried as he pushed my arms away and ran off.

I spoke with John about Matty's fears later that night. He didn't pay much attention, but I noticed after that he began making Matty sit in a corner more frequently instead of pulling off his belt.

John tried to get closer to Em as she grew older. He would tease her and even sing "Buffalo Gals" to get her attention, but to no avail. She maintained her distance and pushed him away if he attempted to hug her. The memory of my beating and losing the baby had driven a solid wedge between them as well. She told me she worried he was crazy and at any given moment might unleash his fury and kill one of us. Emily often spent time away from home with her friends to avoid family conflict. When her education was completed, she worked at a store in town where she met several boys who came courting. John didn't like any of them; no one was good enough for his Em.

***

When Emily was seventeen, she fell in love with Tom, a young farmer who lived down the road closer to Dallas. He seemed ambitious and nice enough, although I'm sure John did as well to my parents when he courted me. I became concerned that Emily wanted to marry him primarily to get away from her father. I sure hoped for her sake that if she did, the years would not change Tom as they had John.

"I can't stand it here any longer, Pa," Emily spoke out to John the day after her eighteenth birthday. "Everyone walks around on eggshells not to upset you." She took a deep breath. "I'm old enough to be on my own, and I'm leaving today."

I glanced at John and saw an icy stare that scared me. He rose from his chair slowly and walked over to Emily, who avoided looking at him until he grabbed her by the shoulders and began shaking her.

"I'll not have a daughter of mine speak to me like that. Where the hell are you goin'?" he shouted.

"To be with Tom. We're planning to marry. His family said I could live with them."

"You're stayin' here. He's not good enough for you. He ain't got nothin'."

"He's a wonderful man, nothing like you. I'd never marry anyone like you!"

Suddenly, John grabbed Emily's arm and began slapping her across the face. When he started to make a fist, I screamed at him to stop while I ran to his gun belt hanging on a hook in the kitchen.

"You'll be so ugly that no man will ever want you except me!" he said as he threw the first punch.

"John, turn around," I shouted. I was holding his pistol, pointed directly at him. "You let her go, or I swear to God I will shoot you."

He loosened his hold on her, and Emily ran from him sobbing as he turned to look at me. I thought he might lunge at me, but he must have thought better of it when he saw my face. I would have shot, perhaps killed, a man I once loved, and he knew it. I didn't want Emily to leave, but it broke my heart to see her so unhappy, so I didn't attempt to make her stay. Emily never lived at home after that, and a few months later, she and Tom married.

When the time came for the wedding, John stoically walked Emily down the aisle and congratulated Tom. Even though he paid lip service to the wedding and left shortly after the ceremony, he allowed me to purchase some necessities for their home as a nice wedding present.

***

Now that Emily was married, I considered leaving John. I talked it over with Tom's father, Jack, who was the local Methodist minister. John and I had been fighting that morning over Owen's returning to school, and I was in a bit of a frenzy when I went into the church.

"Hi, Rebecca," Jack said as he put his arm around me. "Let's go into the back where it will be more private."

He ushered me into his small office and pulled over a chair from the corner so we could sit face to face. "Now, what was it you wanted to talk to me about?"

"Jack, this is confidential, right?"

"Absolutely."

"Well." I hesitated. "John and I haven't been getting along for some time."

"I'm very sorry to hear that, Rebecca." I could tell by his somber look that he truly was.

"I was hoping you could help me decide if I should leave John."

"Sounds like a tall order. Why do you want to leave?"

"I'm so tired of him," I blurted out before I realized what I was saying.

Jack smiled slightly. "Please go on."

"I'm so unhappy. For fifteen years I've watched him beat the boys. I'm tired of the fights, the shouting, and the drama. Now that Em's gone, there's no one to confide in. John likes our business kept private, so I don't dare talk to my women friends. Did Em tell you? I almost shot him when he went after her?"

"Indeed, she did."

"It was a mother's instinct. I would rather he'd been punching me than her."

"Where would you go?"

"I'd take Matty and go back to my parents' home in Philadelphia. The older boys can take care of themselves. I've already talked to them about it, and I know Em and Tom will be there for them if they need help."

"It seems you've decided."

"I've never been very religious. Is it a bad thing for a wife to leave her husband?"

"It's admirable that you take your vows seriously, but you have to feel right in your heart about your decision. God speaks to you through the heart. What does your heart tell you to do?"

I barely paused. "I have to leave, if only for a while. I feel like I will die if I stay here much longer."

"Why don't you explain to John that you are leaving to spend some time with your parents? It's been a while since you've seen them, hasn't it?"

"Five years. Dad wanted to come out for Em's wedding but said he couldn't leave the store."

"Sometimes just getting away can help you view a situation with more clarity."

"No doubt it will."

Jack reached out and took both of my hands as we prayed together.

***

John caught me packing late one morning when he returned home unexpectedly.

"What's all this?" he asked as he looked around our bedroom.

"John, I've given it a lot of thought. I'm going away for a while, back east to see my parents. They're getting older and—"

"What the hell are you sayin'? Are you walkin' away

from our marriage?" His shocked expression grew into a frown.

"I just can't live with you any longer. I've had all I can take of your temper, like when you seem to lose your mind and suddenly punch or take a swing at somebody, usually for no good reason. Not just with us, but with your workers, your friends, and—"

"What'd I do now?" he said, with an annoyed look on his face.

"It's not now; it's the last ten or fifteen years of being afraid of what will happen next. You changed after your father died. I worry constantly that you will accidently kill one of us, or someone else. What would we do if you went to jail? And I could never forgive you if you seriously hurt one of the children. I just don't understand it. I didn't grow up with violence, and I'm miserable living here with you."

"That's just the way it is out here," he said in a nasty tone. "Life's rough; violence is the only way to make things work. Your problem is your parents coddled you too damn much. They already had money and never understood the real world and how hard it is to make a living."

"Yes, my family inherited some money. But my father didn't make us any richer by sitting on his ass or beating anybody up. He's an intelligent businessman. Indeed, I do have a problem, but I'm taking steps to solve it, something I now wish I'd done years ago—returning to the sensibility of the East, where most men are gentlemen and ladies are not treated like farm hands!" I was irritated that he had dragged my parents into our discussion.

John flashed me a look of anger, and I stared back at him while he yanked out a chair from under the table. After sitting down and looking at the kitchen floor for what seemed like an eternity, he closed his eyes and sighed. When he finally glanced up at me, there was little sign of the rage that had simmered in his brown eyes only moments before.

"I know our life together's been a disappointment to you, Becky, but I want you to know that it's never been for me. Not one minute of it. Will you give it another try? I promise you I will change."

"John, I just can't," I whispered. "Twenty years with you has been a mixed blessing. There were good times, wonderful ones even, but the bad times were horrible—watching my children being beaten, losing our baby, your jealous rages. I owe it to Matty and to myself to live in a place without fear of abuse. You had all these years to stop, and you didn't."

"I still love you, Bec," he mumbled. "I don't know what else to say."

I watched his eyes glimmer with disappointment, and it surprised me when I saw a tear or two forming. My heart softened a bit, but I knew John was powerless to change his ways.

Matty and I boarded the stagecoach to St. Louis two days later. Once we were a few miles from home, Matty told me how glad he was that we had left.

Although I felt a tremendous sense of relief as well, my heart ached for months to come because I had left my other precious sons behind.

CHAPTER 7

Not seeing Mother and Papa for years at a time was a sad consequence of living so far away. Although I had a few friends nearby in Dallas, it didn't replace the loving connections with my parents, cousins, and dear friends. The trip west became easier with the new train lines, but Mother and Pa had visited only three times in twenty years.

Sleeping back in my childhood bedroom seemed almost surreal. At first, I lay awake for long periods of time, thinking about John and the boys, wondering if I'd done the right thing. I didn't know when I would return, but I realized I had to at some point, if only for the children.

Everyone was delighted to see Matty and me. Mother cooked many delicious dinners for our relatives and friends to spend time with us. However, as fall approached, I worried that my parents would inquire about my plans for a return trip. I also needed to register Matty for school, but I was ashamed to face Papa—I felt like a failure. Most couples stayed together no matter how difficult it became. He had sacrificed a lot to move us to Texas, and I felt that I had let him down. After two months, I told Mother.

"You have to be wondering why I'm still here."

"I thought you would tell me when you were ready, Becky. It's been a joy to have you and Matty here. It's such a pleasure getting to know one of my grandchildren. Are you leaving soon?"

"That's just it, Mother. I'm not, at least not for some time."

Her hazel eyes widened. "I see."

"No, you don't. I've left John. He changed, Mother. He's angry all the time, and he whips the boys. He punched Emily just before she left and married Tom. He's the reason I lost the last baby. He beat me very badly. It was only once, but I was in pain for days."

"This doesn't sound like John."

"Don't you believe me?" I said, tears coming into my eyes.

"I don't understand it, Becky. I thought you still loved him. Maybe you misinterpreted his actions. Did you or the children provoke him?"

"Mother, John is not the man I married!"

"Men change as time goes on. Your father hasn't been the same since we moved back from Texas, and we're still together. I suppose I've changed too."

I sat there, incredulous that she could not understand what I was trying to explain.

Mother was staring into space and slowly spoke

the words that defined the way she lived much of her life. "What am I going to tell everyone?"

Papa appeared out of nowhere. I was unaware that he had come home for lunch and froze with fear.

"Jane, why don't you go into the kitchen and fix something for lunch?"

"Yes, Dan. Rebecca can use some fatherly advice," she said as she walked out of the room.

"Come here, Becky," he said and took me into his arms. By then I was sobbing uncontrollably.

"I wish you had talked to me first. Your mother has had some health problems. About a year ago, she had a stroke. At first, she had some memory loss and minor impairment of her right arm and leg. Thank goodness she's fine physically now. But her personality's just not the same, and her emotional responses are inappropriate at times."

"Oh, Pa, I'm so sorry. I wish you had told me. I guess I've been so wrapped up in my own problems, I hadn't noticed anything different about her."

"I didn't want you to worry from so far away. Actually, she seems much better now that you're home." He smiled. "But it sounds like you've been keeping secrets too—big ones, Becky. I know some men here who hit their wives, but I never understood it. Still don't. My dear daughter, I want you to be safe!"

"I know, Papa, but I've been worrying that you'd think I gave up too easily. You taught me to see things through even when the going got tough."

"Certainly not when this degree of physical violence is concerned."

"And now Mother's judging me."

"Don't worry about her right now, Becky. You can stay for as long as you wish. What about Owen and Josiah?"

"They're almost as tall as John, and I'm sure they can take care of themselves, physically at least. Besides, Em lives a few miles down the road and would gladly welcome them into her home if need be."

"Rebecca, if it becomes necessary, I will go there myself and bring them here. In the meantime, how about coming back to work with me in the store?"

Papa had that glint in his eye which made him hard to refuse. I remembered how sad he'd become when he was forced to close the store in Texas. Since then, we'd never discussed his broken dream of us working together.

"Yes, Papa, for now, at least," I said. He smiled as he leaned over and kissed me on the cheek.

***

Several months later, the sleepless nights returned. Emily was now in her sixth month of pregnancy. The two thousand miles separating us had stretched even longer. Em didn't say it in her letters, but I could tell she was apprehensive. I understood this was the reason she and Tom were inviting me to move in with them for a while. It was a hard decision because Papa had become dependent on me to manage the store inventory, and many painful memories with John still lingered. Regardless, my heart wouldn't let me stay away much longer from Em and the two sons I loved so dearly. A year was time enough.

CHAPTER 8

Matty was eleven now and seemed pleased to be returning to Texas. He had done surprisingly well in school that year—almost at the top of his class—but he often mentioned how much he missed his older brothers and Emily. No doubt, he even missed his father. Isn't it strange, how kids seem to love their parents no matter what they do to them? Of course, it wasn't all bad. John had shown him and his brothers some kindness despite the abuse. Matty received the worst of it, though. By the time he came along, John was working long hours and drinking way too much. Of all my children, Matty looked the most like John. I often wondered if he felt as though he was punishing himself when he hit Matty.

After a tearful goodbye, our train arrived in St. Louis four days later. I remember how much I dreaded the dry, dusty stagecoach ride from there into Texas. I was sure glad it didn't rain. There's nothing worse than being stuck out in the middle of nowhere with mud halfway up the wheels. I sure looked forward to the day when the railway would be totally completed into Dallas.

Emily and Tom met us at the station. I was thrilled to see Em running toward me, the way she did as a child, with that long, brown hair trailing in the wind. I couldn't believe that she had grown so quickly into this lovely, pregnant woman.

"Oh, Mama, it's been much too long," Emily exclaimed as she threw her arms around my neck. Tears streamed down her face.

"I know, my dear daughter. I'm so, so happy to see you again."

While Emily was greeting her brother, I glanced over at Tom who stood there looking a bit shy. I put my arm around him, and he gave me a quick hug. "Looks like you're taking good care of my girl. She looks healthy and so happy, too."

"I'm doin' my best, ma'am."

"Please call me Ma, or Becky, even."

"I will," he said, smiling. "And I want you to know you're both welcome to stay with us for as long as you like. Em has missed you somethin' terrible."

"I really appreciate the invitation, Tom." I'd liked Tom from the first day I'd met him. He was four years older than Emily and decidedly more mature and sincere than the others who had come courting.

"I invited Pa and the boys over for dinner," Emily said, as we climbed into the buggy. "I hope that's okay, the part about Papa, I mean."

I remember how my stomach muscles tightened as

I thought about John. It seemed almost too soon to face him again. A flash of panic shot through me as I suddenly wondered if I had made a big mistake by returning to Texas.

"Well, I have to see him eventually. It might as well be today."

***

I was overjoyed at the sight of Owen and Josiah. At the ages of sixteen and fifteen, they weren't much for writing, and it had been a few months since I'd heard from either of them. I could tell from the look in their eyes and their quick, shy hugs they were glad to see me as well. It struck me hard how long I'd been away when I realized Owen had to be taller than his father.

John came through the door just as we finished putting food on the table. A few silver threads now mixed with his jet-black hair.

"Hi, Becky," he said, with a glance at me and then at the table. "This sure looks mighty good."

"Sit down next to me, Papa," Emily said, "so I can make sure you get enough to eat."

John's timing had been perfect. I had only a chance to respond with, "Hi, John," before we all sat down, and Tom said the blessing. He had learned how to say a nice blessing from his father.

During the meal, awkward silences fueled an uneasy tension between John and me. Finally, I asked him, "How's the cattle business?"

"Been a bit of a struggle, Bec. I had to hire a trail boss to replace me on some drives 'cause I didn't wanna leave the boys alone so much, so that's kinda cut into the cash flow. But we're makin' it work. Right, boys?"

"We're doing mighty fine, Ma," Owen responded. "I quit school after you left, but Josiah's still goin'. I even learned how to cook some." He grinned. "But it don't taste like yours did."

"Nothin' tastes like Mom's cooking, but Em's is real good," Josiah said with a quick grin at his sister.

"You're growin' like a weed, boy," John said to Matty.

"I reckon I am, Pa. I'll soon be as tall as Owen."

"Becky, thanks for bringin' him back to me."

I noticed the surprised look on Matty's face. "Boys need their fathers too," I said.

Pangs of guilt shot through me during dinner. It saddened me that John had allowed Owen to quit school, and I thought about how different things might have been if I had stayed. We had a very dedicated schoolmarm at our small school on the prairie. She welcomed the children up to age sixteen. I sometimes taught the class when she needed help or was sick. I wondered if I still could, because working with children was something I thoroughly enjoyed.

Suddenly, there was a knock at the door, and Tom's parents, Jack and Mabel, walked in.

"I hope we're not comin' at a bad time," Mabel said as she handed a lemon pie to Emily. "Jack thought we should give you a day or two, but I just couldn't wait to welcome back your mother, Emily."

"Sit down. I was just going to put dessert out," Em said, looking a little flustered. Tom jumped up to get more chairs.

"It's nice to see you both again," I said.

"Same here," Jack said. "And I know how happy Emily and Tom are that you're here."

"I hope you're stayin' a while," Mabel said. "These men could use a good meal or two. I've been taking food over to them once a week."

I wondered if she thought I was moving back in with John. "I'll be staying with Emily while I'm here, but I'll do what I can."

Mabel gave me a blank stare. I quickly began picking up some dishes. "Please excuse me. I need to help Emily in the kitchen," I said.

"This is getting more awkward by the minute," I said to Emily as I put the dishes on the counter.

"I'm sorry, Mama. I didn't expect them to come today." Just then, Tom walked into the kitchen with a few more plates.

"I'll try to move things along," he said, grabbing some silverware to take into the dining room.

As we walked back to the table, Mabel remarked, "My, isn't Tom quite the host, even doing women's work these days."

We sat there in silence, munching on pieces of apple and lemon pies. Soon, Jack and Tom began talking about the fall harvest, and John chimed in. Emily and Mabel discussed pumpkin pie recipes, while I nodded and tried to figure out why I found Mabel so annoying. I hadn't when I lived there before, but I had only been in her company a few times. Besides, she was gracious enough to offer Emily a home when she left ours. I decided that maybe she was always like that, and I just hadn't noticed. I knew I was overly tired and perhaps more sensitive than usual. No doubt though, she was fortunate to be married to Jack. He seemed a genuinely kind man.

Tom soon excused himself from the table, and John then asked if he could speak with me in the parlor. Even talking with John alone seemed a welcome change from the uneasiness I felt around Mabel.

"Thought you might like a break," John said with a grin. He surprised me with his sensitivity, and I found it easy to smile back at him.

"It's good to see you, Bec. I wasn't sure if I ever would again."

"I had to come back for Emily, and to see the boys."

"I reckoned you didn't come for me, but I'm real happy to see you. Can I give you a hug?"

I took a step back. "No, John, not now."

He looked a little disappointed. "I understand, really I do. I was wonderin' why you never answered my letters. Did you get them?"

"Yes. I didn't know what to say to you. I had so many awful memories from those last few years that I wanted to put behind me. I'm sorry, John. I didn't mean to hurt you more."

"If it makes you feel any better, I haven't beat up on anyone for a few months now."

"Even the boys?"

"Nope. Haven't touched them since you left. You can ask them."

John walked closer and put his hands on my shoulders. "Goin' back home was good for you, Becky. You don't look so tired and worried anymore. How are your parents doin'?"

"It was wonderful to spend time with them. Mama had a spell of poor health for a bit, but they were both well when I left."

"I'm glad to hear that. Do you think—"

"John, I'm really tired now. We'll talk again soon, I promise. I just heard Mabel and Jack leave, and I need to help Em clean up before I turn in."

"Okay, Bec. I'll see you later, then."

That night, I lay awake thinking back on the day. I was pleased to see Emily so happy. It reminded me of myself during my first year with John. I so hoped that Tom and Emily would always be in love, and that God would bless their marriage until their days ended. It warmed my heart that to see that John and Em had become closer, too.

Seeing the boys looking happy and healthy was a

special joy. Em told me while we were making dinner that the boys had grown closer to each other as well as to her after I left. She said that John was sullen and withdrawn at first and left them mostly on their own. Later, he stopped drinking and became kinder. It seemed my leaving had been a blessing in disguise. I no longer worried that John would hit Matty.

You know, it wasn't even so bad seeing John. I felt relieved to get it over with. I just hoped he wouldn't try to get me to move back into the house.

Chapter 9

Two days before Christmas, Emily's labor began. Her water broke while she was baking in the kitchen. I jumped up and ran to her when I heard her piercing scream. Tom had gone to help his father decorate the church for the Christmas Eve service.

"Let's get you into bed," I said walking her into her bedroom.

"But, Ma, the mess—"

"Don't worry. I'll clean up. Put on a nightgown so you can get in bed. Do you have any pains yet?"

"No, not yet. I'm a little scared, Mama. I'm so glad you're here."

"This is all normal. My water broke first, both with you and Owen."

"I've been wantin' to ask you something, Ma," Emily said with hesitation. "Did all your babies live except the one you lost when Pa beat you?"

"Yes, darlin'." The truth was that a year after Emily's birth, I had lost one full-term boy shortly after birth.

"I sure wish Tom would come home. I think he's gonna be a couple more hours."

It concerned me because she wasn't due until late in January, but I did all I could to reassure her. Tom came home at noon, and by then, Emily was having hard labor pains. I told him to go fetch the doctor. They returned an hour later. Six hours of hard labor passed, and my precious grandson was born with the cord wrapped around his neck. His lifeless body lay beside his mother who had passed out from pain after the final thrust.

I wandered into the parlor where Tom sat with his head in his hands. Dr. Templeton had shared the sad news on his way out. John was there also because Tom had left him a note at home on his way to the doctor's.

I noticed the tear stains on Tom's cheeks as he looked up at me. "Can I go in?"

"Yes, but she doesn't know yet. She passed out, and Doc said to let her rest. She really had quite a time of it." I put my hand on his shoulder. "Tom, I'm so sorry. I don't know what else to say."

"I don't understand it, Ma. I guess God wanted it that way." He shook his head as he got up and slowly headed toward the bedroom.

I glanced at John sitting there in silence, staring out the window. He suddenly blurted out, "This happened because Tom made her work too hard these last couple of months. Doing all that canning and then the sewing for the Christmas pageant that his lazy mother should have been—"

"John, this does no good. Just let it be in God's hands."

"I'm gonna' tell him when he comes out that—"

Emily's cries from the bedroom startled both of us. I grabbed John's arm as he leaped out of the chair. "Please don't! It'll just hurt everyone. Do you want to hurt Emily?"

"It's not right, Bec. She should've never married him."

"Your bitterness will push her away from you. You shouldn't force her to choose again. Is that what you want?"

"No, because I'd lose. I always do. Tell Em I'll see her later," John shouted as he stormed out.

Emily was devastated by the loss of her first child. The next day, she and Tom buried little James in a grave next to Rev. Elwood's church and began to move on with their lives, determined to have another baby soon. Em had a lot of stitches and needed to rest some. The Christmas holidays passed quietly. I did all the cooking and cleaning I could to help, and by New Year's she was almost back to normal.

***

The next month flew by. Matty had been sleeping at John's house most of the time. He loved going to school with Josiah. Once a week, I went over and cooked some of their favorites, but it felt strange—so many memories, both good and bad, floated around in that ranch house. Whenever John came home, I usually found an excuse to leave as soon as I could. Dreams of living there again began to invade my sleep.

By now, I knew the primary reason I came to Dallas had passed and wondered if I should leave. I worried that John would draw me back into a life with him if I stayed much longer. He attempted to make me feel guilty about how much the children needed me, and I was fearful that I might give into it. I didn't want to intrude on Emily and Tom's life, either. At this point, I continued to feel welcomed, but I hoped Tom wouldn't come to resent me.

I began to feel lost between two worlds. Philadelphia no longer seemed like home. The twenty years that passed had put too much time and distance between me and the old friends and relatives I had loved so dearly. Moreover, I dreaded when anyone outside the immediate family asked questions I didn't want to answer. I knew I couldn't return—at least not yet.

I was becoming increasingly annoyed that Mabel got a dig in every time she could about how I should go back living with John and take care of my family. At first, I thought it was because she resented cooking and taking food to them, but I soon realized she was being judgmental. I had once believed, too, that a wife should stay with her husband until death, no matter what. Fifteen years of seeing my children beaten and living with fear and anger had changed all that. I had learned the hard way that love is not always enough.

The good Reverend never commented on my living situation. Most of the time, he had trouble getting a word into any conversation when his wife was present.

After much deliberation, I decided to stay until the following January. Both Tom and Emily reassured me that I was more than welcome in their home for as long as I wanted to be there.

***

I was startled when John invited me to go out for dinner on Valentine's Day. I was reluctant to accept, but the second time he asked, I agreed. He showed up with a lovely bouquet, and we drove to the "Quail's Nest," where we had eaten twice before on special occasions. I marveled at the delicious roast beef they served. Although I was a decent cook, my beef never turned out that tender. To my surprise, I was happy being out with John. It seemed almost like the early days of our marriage when he had been more carefree and considerate.

We finished up our wine and headed out. On the way home John put him arm around me. I didn't mind too much because the night air was damp and frosty.

"Bec, I'm havin' a wonderful time. What about you?"

"I'm enjoying myself."

"I've missed you so darn much. Last year was one of the worst of my life with you gone. Now you're back, and I really want us to be together again."

I began shivering, and John stopped the buggy. He pulled me toward him, and the familiarity of his embrace lured me into hugging him back. Soon he tilted my face toward him and kissed me tenderly, unlike the rough or casual kisses in the later years of marriage. "I love you, Bec. Will you come back to me and the children? I've changed. Really, I have."

"I'll think about it, John. Honestly, I will, but I believe this decision needs time, lots of time." A fear of flirting with disaster flashed through me.

Later, I considered it. I realized it would be best for the children to have their mother there cooking, cleaning, and being a part of their everyday lives, but I knew in my heart that this wasn't what I wanted. If John could return to be the same man I married, it might work. I didn't know if he could. Besides, I was damned if I would allow my heart to be broken again.

I put John off—it was nice to be courted. He knew that I had a weakness for romance, and he played that card well.

CHAPTER 10

I'll never forget John's heart-wrenching words: "Owen's been shot."

The room turned white, and I slumped into the nearest chair. "John, what are you saying? What happened?"

"Someone shot him in the back on the edge of the farm. He must have been there a couple of hours before Josiah and Matty found him."

"How badly is he hurt?"

"I'm not sure. Bec. We must go to him. He's at Doc Templeton's."

I grabbed my shawl, left Emily a note, and we rushed over. The doctor had already operated to get the bullet out, and Owen was still sedated.

"I don't like the way he's breathing. I got the bullet out fine, but it punctured his lung on the way through." He shook his head. "I can't stop the bleeding."

John and I looked at each other in disbelief. I glanced over at my sons. They sat stiffly, staring at the floor.

"Can't you do somethin' more, Doc?" John said.

"I'd suggest we pray," Dr. Templeton said.

I heard John sigh.

Closing my eyes, I silently spoke to God asking him to help my boy. A short time later, John broke the silence. "I've been praying too, Becky. I figured it couldn't hurt nothin'."

Doc let us in to see him after a while, but he was still unconscious. Beads of perspiration dotted his forehead as he struggled with each breath. I took his hand. "Mama's here," I whispered softly, kissing his cheek.

John put his hand on Owen's leg. "Your Pa's here too. You're gonna' be just fine, Son."

When his breathing worsened, Doc gave him more morphine to keep him relaxed. At one point, I felt faint and grabbed John's arm.

"Take her into the other room, I'll stay with him," the doctor said.

John guided me to the waiting room. My dam of tears burst loose when I saw Emily and Tom. Emily grabbed me, and we held onto each other until our tears stopped falling.

A short time later, Tom and Emily went in to see him. Soon they returned, looking pale and somber. Em knelt down in front of us. "Mama, Pa, he's gone. Owen's dead."

Her words cut through me. I cradled Em's head in my lap and sat there with my eyes closed. Two minutes later, I heard Matty run out of the office. I looked up to see a tear-stained Josiah running after him.

John jumped up. "I always told you prayin' don't work 'cause there's no God to hear it."

Emily, Tom, and I held hands and began to pray for the salvation of Owen's soul. I thought I heard the door slam again.

***

All the clichés you've heard about a mother losing a child are true. When I brought this strong, young man into life, I never considered him a temporary gift. And yes, it does go against nature for parents to bury a child. It took me a few years to stop questioning God and trust that He had a better plan, even though I would never understand. Owen's death left a deep, hollow place inside my heart that nothing could ever fill.

After the funeral, I started going to Rev. Jack's church regularly. Although I believed in God, my parents had not raised me with religion. I thought it was important for the boys to have that opportunity, so I insisted they go with me.

Josiah had become sullen and withdrawn since Owen's death. After a month, he refused to go, saying he couldn't believe in a god who had taken his brother away. It concerned me when I began seeing much of John's angry ways in him. To the contrary, Matty seemed to find comfort in going to church and enjoyed the camaraderie.

It wasn't long before they arrested Tobias Crane for Owen's murder. He said he thought he shot John. During the trial, it came out that John had been having sexual relations with Mrs. Crane repeatedly for at least two years. Tobias was sentenced to life in prison. John thought they should have hanged him.

It devastated me to learn of John's unfaithfulness. I had allowed him to creep back into my heart and my life, believing he was changing for the better because he had stopped drinking and seemed less prone to violence. Looking back, I guess I never could see clear through to his dark side. I was always trying so hard to find the best in him.

A few days after the trial, Emily and Tom invited John over for dinner. After dessert, Emily stood up with a big smile on her face. "We have news."

"Oh, I'm so thrilled," I said, jumping up and throwing my arms around them both.

"Mama, how did you know what I was going to say? Am I showing?"

"A mother just knows these things by instinct." I smiled. "Besides, I heard you vomiting a few mornings last week."

"When is the child due?" John asked.

"In November, Pa."

"Well, I'm happy for you. Children can be a joy if you handle them right. I hope all goes well this time, Em. I really do. Can I talk to you outside, Bec?"

I hesitated. "Okay."

I remember so well that warm, spring evening. A soft breeze was blowing across my face as John started to put his arms around me. I put my hand up to stop him and stepped back.

"I can't do this anymore."

"Bec, I don't know what to say except I'm sorry. We hadn't had relations in so long that I had to do somethin' about it. I didn't do it to hurt you. Besides, she came on to me the first time. I guess old Tobias wasn't man enough."

"John, I don't want to hear this."

"Bec, it's over now. I don't have no feelins' for her. I never did."

The following few moments of silence were deafening.

"John, what the blazes are you talking about? That's your damn excuse for getting your son killed?" I couldn't believe that he was talking about this in such a matter-of-fact manner.

"Bec, that's not fair. That's not what I'm sayin'. I'm tryin' to apologize. I don't want to ruin what we have."

"John, we no longer have anything between us, except the children."

"Becky, c'mon."

"I'm going inside. It suddenly got very chilly out here."

He grabbed my arm.

"John, let the hell go of me before I do or say something I'll be sorry for."

I ran inside to a startled-looking Emily and Tom. "I'm okay," I said. "I just need to be alone."

When John followed me in a minute later, I heard Emily say, "Pa, not now. I think you'd better leave."

***

Since Owen was killed, Matty was staying full time with me at Emily's unless he was in school. He told me that John had started acting mean again, and he didn't want to be around him. It wasn't too long before Tom found out that John was drinking again. I knew Josiah must have told him. My older son had been stopping over more often, and I was glad that both he and Matty were growing closer to Tom, who had proven himself to be an admirable son-in-law with his maturity and kind ways.

Early one morning, Josiah told us that John hadn't come home the night before. The sheriff had just been at their house asking about him. Tom offered to go to the sheriff's office to try to find out what was going on. Josiah wanted to go with him, but Tom thought it better he go alone. He returned an hour later.

"What happened?" I asked as soon as I saw the serious look on his face.

"Let's sit down." I could tell as he glanced at Emily, he was worried how his news would impact on her pregnancy.

Tom sat between Emily and me on the sofa while my two boys sunk into the loveseat across from us.

"Tom, please," Emily said.

"Okay, well, John is in jail for beating up Nathan Crane."

"Tobias' son?" I asked. Tom nodded.

I glanced over at the boys, not sure what to say. Matty looked like he was about to cry. "Your father sure gets crazy when he drinks."

"No surprise to us, Ma," Josiah mumbled.

"There's more. He almost killed him," said Tom.

"What?" Emily exclaimed.

Tom put his arm around her. "Emily, please calm down. It's already happened. There's nothing we can do about it now except pray."

"I know you're right, Tom. I just need a minute," Emily responded as she wept softly.

I silently said a prayer for Nathan and Mrs. Crane. I knew there was nothing worse than seeing your child lying close to death. Even though she was a willing participant in the adultery, her life was now in shambles, and I couldn't help but feel sorry for her.

***

While John was in jail awaiting his trial, Emily and I kept busy getting ready for the baby. We felt sure that this time everything would go well, but we were all prepared in case it didn't. Some women in the area had recently lost babies at birth or shortly afterward. One day, I admitted to her I'd lost the child she didn't know about.

"I'm glad you finally told me, Mama. I wish I'd been older though, so I could have helped you through it," she said. "Did Pa console you?"

"A little, but he was mad more than anything—at God, I guess."

I walked over to Emily and wrapped my arms around her. "My beautiful daughter, you are such an old soul. How was I ever so lucky to have you for my child? You were with me when I lost the second one—you'll never know how much that meant to me."

Fortunately, Nathan began to recover from his injuries. John, however, was sentenced to two years in prison because of the brutality of the attack. A neighbor purchased our house, property, and John's share of the business during that time. John didn't want to sell, but he had no choice since there was no one he could depend on to take over the ranch. He and his brother, Chester, had grown apart over the years and no longer spoke to each other.

There were many debts to pay off, and creditors came calling when they learned of John's sentencing. I was happy that I could retrieve my collection of books and a few personal items before the house sold. After the payoffs, John put the remainder of the money in an account in my name to keep it safe. I hoped there would be some left after he got out of prison to give to the boys when they were older for their education, or when they got married.

Tom and Rev. Jack were so gracious in helping to negotiate these matters with John because they did not want Emily or me to go repeatedly to the jail. They even took the boys to visit John twice. There came a deep sadness for them though, in October, when Mabel passed away suddenly. The doctor said it must have been a heart attack.

Tom's grief soon turned to happiness when our little Henrietta was born shortly before Thanksgiving. That precious eight-pound, blue-eyed bundle of love brought much happiness to us all. Money was tight—Tom had six of us to feed now. Late in the summer, I'd taken a job at a dress shop in town, but it was to end in January. Tom told me not to worry. He believed that God would take care of us, and I'd be darned if he didn't. As time went on, we found there was almost as much food to go around as there was love in that small house.

CHAPTER 11

Christmas 1882 was one I would always remember. It was bitterly cold when we went to the Christmas Eve service at Jack's church. Rev. Jack was very popular, and people often crammed into the church and lined up against the back wall to hear his words. I marveled at what a wonderful speaker he was. He didn't preach down to us; he uplifted us as he talked about the meaning of love and other gifts of the spirit. Jack came back to the house with us that night because Tom didn't want him to be alone.

Em and I got out of bed before dawn to get started on Christmas dinner. When the boys woke up, we all went into the parlor to exchange gifts. A small pinyon pine stood in the corner, decorated with red bows, crocheted snowflakes, and some of my precious, glass ornaments from back East. It was crowned with a lovely, china angel. Gifts tied with brightly colored ribbons surrounded its base.

"Please open mine first," I said.

I remember being so excited as I handed a package to everyone and was eager to see if they liked their gifts, especially Tom and Jack. Men's shirts were not my favorite items to sew. I had been very busy for the last several months making clothes for everyone—a task I considered a fine emotional outlet for all the drama experienced during the year.

"Oh, Ma, this dress is beautiful. Thank you so much." Emily got up and hugged me. "And when did you have time to make all these darling things for Henrietta?"

"I have been very busy; I have to admit." I smiled and glanced over at the men who seemed to like their shirts. The boys and Tom came up and kissed me. Soon Jack walked over with packages in his hand for Emily and me.

"I hope you like these," he said, looking as if he wanted to say more. Emily opened hers first. Inside were two silver hair combs; one was decorated in mother-of-pearl.

"Oh, how lovely—"

"They belonged to Mabel. I bought them for her when we were courting, but I don't think she ever wore them. I hope you don't mind that—"

"My goodness, no. I love them." She took one and carefully slid it through her long hair on the right side. "How do I look?"

"Beautiful, Em, as always, but even more so now," Tom said. He leaned over and gave his wife a kiss.

Everyone was looking at me now as I opened the tiny box and found a beautiful, cameo pin. It had the face of a lovely woman on it. I looked up into Jack's twinkling, blue eyes. "This is exquisite. I really do love it, Jack."

"I hope that's true. It reminded me of you." He quickly added, "It's in the same box as the day I gave it to Mabel. I don't think she ever took it out. I never did very well at pleasing her."

"Pa, I don't think any of us did too well at that," Tom said, staring at the floor. "Ma had such high expectations about everything, it seemed. I think that's why she wasn't often very happy."

"I believe you're right, Son. Anyway, I shipped most of her valuables back to the girls in Virginia, but I kept these for the two of you," he said.

"I'm honored you gave this to me, Jack." I truly was even though I sometimes did not have the kindest feelings for Mabel. I stood up and gave him a quick kiss on the cheek.

A few seconds later, Jack said, "Is it me, or is it hot in here?" He unbuttoned the top button of his shirt. Everyone laughed, and I noticed Emily and Tom glance at each other and smile.

Later we feasted on chicken, venison, and pork. I still remember the huge bowls of mashed potatoes, greens, applesauce, and other fixins that Emily and I made. Em's delicious apple pie and my lemon pound cake were the dessert favorites. It had been a perfect day. I was beginning to feel that I truly belonged in Texas once again. I went to bed that night happier than I had been in years.

***

In February, we received word from the prison that John was ill and not expected to live very long. They were releasing him so he could come home to die. No one had seen him since the holidays, and this came as a big shock. The children, who each had their own mixed feelings about John, were distraught.

"We have to bring him here, Ma," Emily said with tears in her eyes.

"But where can we put him?"

"We'll put a bed in the parlor. I'll talk to Tom about it."

I already knew Tom would agree to it. He and Jack went into town to pick up John a few days later. I remember there were snowflakes falling as they pulled up in the buggy. It startled me how yellow John was when I first saw him. He seemed in pain and barely looked at any of us. Em and I went in to talk with him first.

"Pa, I'm glad you're here. I'm sorry I don't have a bedroom to offer you. "

"It's fine, Em, and wipe those tears off your face, girl. I'm not dead yet."

"Will you both excuse me? I think I hear Henrietta. I'll be back soon." I could tell John's words had stung her.

"Is there anything you need, John?"

"Other than a new body, no, Becky." He went on, "I don't like to have to be here, but they seemed to think

I should be with family. Lettin' a prisoner out of jail to die. How noble of them."

He looked up at me when I didn't respond. "Bec, you know I don't like havin' no control over what's happenin' to me."

"I can understand that you're angry," I said. "But I hope you'll be a little more gracious to Tom and Emily. It is their house."

"We had a house once where I could've gone. I'd have felt like I was at home with you and my young'uns around me in a house I'd built myself. Bec, none of this would be happenin' if you hadn't left."

I felt myself becoming angry, but I think I remained somewhat stone-faced. I wasn't going to argue with a dying man. I said," Is there anything else you need?"

"No, the only thing I really need, I can't have—you, Becky."

"I'll talk to you later, John." I turned and walked out the door.

John lasted another two weeks and passed away peacefully. During that time, his moods switched from anger to sorrow. He apologized to each of us for ways he had hurt us in the past—things I didn't realize he'd been aware of. It made me sad to believe he was crueler than I thought because deep down he seemed to know better. Or maybe, it was just his awareness had grown because he was older and dying. At the very end, I started to see some of the finer qualities he had shown me in the early years of our marriage.

Apparently when he stared death in the face, it freed him from his anger.

John Coulter died at the age of forty-eight. Rev. Jack gave a real nice sermon, and we buried him in the family plot next to his little grandson. Even Chester showed up to pay his respects to the family. John had been the love of my life, and I had to admit to myself that pieces of him still lived deeply within my heart. It was a connection that could not be severed and would remain with me for the rest of my life. I felt relieved now that he was at peace. We all continued to grieve for some time, each in our own way.

By summer, I was thinking that the boys and I should move out. I had saved some money and was beginning to look for a place. Tom said he hoped we wouldn't go. The boys could continue to earn their keep working on the farm plus he was happy to have us there for Emily's sake. He stressed how much he enjoyed the warmth of our family life together—a warmth, he said, he'd never experienced before.

Chapter 12

I was mighty surprised when Jack asked me out to dinner for my birthday in July. We drove all the way into Dallas to a fancy restaurant.

"What a nice place, Jack," I said, staring across the table at his smiling face. "Have you been here before?"

"No, never. I heard about it and thought I'd like to come here for a special occasion." He glanced down at the table and then peered up at me. "I'm not sure how to say this, but—Becky, can I court you?"

"Uh, yes. I guess so." The more I thought about it, the more I realized I did have fond feelings for Jack. I enjoyed his company very much.

"Dang! That's a relief. It worried me I was being presumptuous and that you'd say no. Rebecca, you're the most charming woman I've ever had the pleasure to be in the company of. I'd love to know you better."

I smiled. "Jack, I'd enjoy getting to know you better, I'm sure of that."

***

I soon came to know a kindness and gentleness I'd never experienced with a man. He saw the best in everyone, even me. I worried that the years in Texas had hardened me and somehow made me less of a lady. No longer was I the naïve, young woman with visions of marrying a cowboy. When I expressed my fears to him two months later, I was shocked at his response.

"You're right. Life changes people. I don't think I would have fallen in love with that fancy, young woman, but I'm fiercely attracted to this captivating, mature woman who stands in front of me now. Becky, I'm deeply in love with you."

It took me a minute to respond. When I was ready, I looked into his eyes as I said softly, "I do love you, Jack."

To trust and allow another man into my heart was not something I expected so soon. But how could I not love a man who put his heart and soul into helping others with such passion? He even managed to understand me in a way John never could. I was hooked. In November, we became engaged, and Jack gave me an exquisite ring with seven tiny pearls clustered around a sparkling, round diamond. He made sure I knew it hadn't belonged to Mabel, saying he had called in some favors to purchase it.

***

It was a thrill to have my parents return for the wedding in April. On the morning of the big day, Mother helped me into my ivory dress, as she had on the day I married John.

"Another beautiful creation, Becky. Did you ever consider making wedding gowns to sell? You know how I worry about that talent going to waste."

"Please stop worrying, Mother. All these years I've been making the family's clothes, and now I will be redecorating Jack's house—our house, rather. He told me I could do whatever I wanted with it."

Suddenly I thought I was going to faint. Small beads of sweat began forming on my forehead. "I have to sit down," I said.

"Becky, are you okay? I'll go get your father."

"No, just get Emily. Please."

"Ma, what's happening?" Em said as she rushed in. "You're so pale."

"I'm all right. I'm not sure I can do this."

"Do what?" Mother asked.

"Marry Jack. I don't know if I love him enough."

"Oh?" Mother said.

"Mama, you're probably just nervous. Jack loves you very much. I overheard him talking about you to Tom the other night. He feels things for you he never felt before."

"Well, that's reassuring. I wish I could say the same about him. It's not that I don't love him. I do. But I worry it's not enough to spend the rest of my life with him."

"Becky, you're not getting any younger, and decent men are hard to find. Aside from being a preacher, I feel he's good man. You know I wouldn't say so if I didn't believe it."

"I know, Mother."

"I expect the two of you will come to love each other more deeply as time goes on."

Mother often seemed to have a sixth sense about the future, so I took her words to heart along with Emily's, and married Jack that day.

The deacon performed the ceremony in Jack's church. Emily and Tom stood as our witnesses, and Jack's older children, Carol and Richard, were there from Virginia along with their families. Josiah even brought one of his girlfriends. Seventeen-month-old Henrietta upstaged me when Matty walked her down the aisle as she waved a small bouquet of flowers at everyone.

Em and Tom put together a nice spread of food at their home. Since Emily was five months pregnant, several of our guests were quick to offer help, and it turned out to be a lovely occasion.

I was delighted that my parents had made the trip there. Papa said he would never miss a wedding of mine, although he hoped this would be the last one. It was a thrill for me to see both my parents with Henrietta, as well. My father even sat on the floor and rolled a ball back and forth to her as he had once with me. I burst into tears when they left two days later and tried not to think about how each time I saw them, they looked a bit older.

***

My life as Rebecca Coulter had ended now at the age of forty-eight. Becky Elwood opened a brand-new chapter with different hopes and dreams. I looked forward to life with this fifty-two-year-old preacher in a solid, loving partnership. Isn't it funny, how when old dreams die, unexpected new ones spring up to take their place?

Perhaps, you are wondering about the wedding night. Quite frankly, I wasn't sure I wanted to consummate our marriage that first night. I got into my red, lace nightgown, wishing I hadn't made one as provocative. John's eyes got big when he saw me.

"My goodness, Becky. You take my breath away. That's such a beautiful gown, and you look ravishing in it."

"I was wishing after I made it that I had done it in white or ivory. Do I look like a prostitute?"

"Sweetheart, you could never look like a prostitute, even if you tried. Your lovely, angelic face would scare away the customers. To the contrary, your loveliness is driving this preacher crazy."

I giggled. "Do you mind if I go sit and read a little?"

"If you'd like...but we could talk about it if you're

feeling apprehensive." It made me sad to see the glimmer of disappointment in his eyes.

"I just need a few minutes to relax by myself. It's been a long day."

"Of course, it has. No expectations. It would be nice to hold you before we go to sleep."

I soon changed my mind and got in bed with Jack. He held me until the scent of his maleness began to arouse me. I began kissing him and lovingly stroking his body. He let me take the lead, and our lovemaking turned out to be one of the most sensual and satisfying I had ever experienced. With John, there had been more fire and passion, but it seemed more about sex than love. I now felt the love that this dear man had for me in undeniable ways. It was a love that I would discover to be steadfast and comforting in the days and years to come.

CHAPTER 13

O ne morning, four months later, Jack answered the door and came back with a telegram in his hand and a frown on his face.

"It's addressed to you, Becky."

I stared at him. "Open it, please, Jack."

He glanced at it and sighed.

"What is it?"

Jack sat beside me. "Your father had a heart attack." He hesitated. "He's gone, Becky. I'm so sorry."

"No, oh my God, no." After I caught my breath, I began to sob.

Jack took me into his arms and held me until the pain eased a bit.

"Jack, I have to go to my mother."

"I understand, Becky, and I'll go with you."

His words were comforting. "But how can you take the time away?"

"I'll find someone. Perhaps the elders or even a visiting preacher will fill in. Don't you worry about it. Just get us packed."

Next to the day Owen died, this was the worst day of my life. My father was my rock. He had taught me to be strong and persistent, yet kind. He was the reason I had the gumption to follow my dreams.

We arrived in time for the funeral. The conflux of Papa's friends, business associates, customers, and relatives who came to pay their respects to a man they highly regarded was a comfort to Mother and me. I heard new stories of his kindnesses and how he stood by others in times of need. It did not surprise me when we learned later that Papa owed a sizeable amount to creditors. It was so like him to put people ahead of business.

Jack had to leave within a few days after the funeral to get back to his church. I stayed because Mother was still beside herself and needed someone to be with her and to handle the business matters. We decided to sell the business to Papa's nephew, Kevin, who had been working there since I returned to Texas.

"What am I going to do without him, Becky? I don't know how to live without him. I fear I will follow him shortly."

"Mother, you're a strong woman. You'll be fine with your friends and family so close by."

She shook her head. "Humph, they are slowly dying off, too."

"Papa left you enough money for the rest of your life so you can live here as long as you'd like. Or, if you want to come back to Texas with me, you are welcome—"

"I will never return to that god-forsaken place as long as I live!"

I hadn't realized Mother disliked Texas that strongly. "Well, just know that you have family in that god-forsaken place who love you very much."

"A lot of good that does."

"Mother, I'll try to visit more often."

"Trying doesn't get it done."

I stood up. "Then I will do it!"

"I won't hold my breath!"

Since we were already at odds, I blurted out, "Mother, I've been here over two months now. I need to return to my husband who is patiently waiting for me. I have a ticket for a train on Friday."

She glared at me. "I curse the day we moved you to Texas!"

I walked out of the parlor and into my bedroom, where I cried softly. The next day Mother was in a lighter mood, and she agreed that it was the right thing for me to return to Jack. Her sisters and their children had promised me that they would look in on her and take her out regularly. I did visit Mother the following year.

***

It thrilled me to see Jack again, but I was shocked to find his daughter, Carol, had moved into our home thirty days after Jack returned. Although, I knew that he loved me very much, it wasn't long before I realized that Jack couldn't defend me to her. He was simply too kind to everyone.

We had spent the month following the wedding, decorating the house. I was so proud of the furniture I'd reupholstered and the new drapes and curtains I'd sewn. Jack and I even replaced much of the wallpaper. Mabel's dark, drab tans and browns had now vanished. A lighter, cheerier look with blues and greens dotted the parlor and our bedroom. I knew Jack liked green, so I added it wherever I could. He said it reminded him of the God's green earth in Virginia that he often missed.

The trouble started when Carol said to me, "I see you changed everything. Is this appropriate for a minister's house? These satin drapes look more like a brothel."

"I'm sure it's fine," Jack muttered.

"You are very talented, Rebecca. You made these, didn't you?" Carol said.

"Yes, I did." I resisted the urge to inquire as to how she would know what a brothel's drapes might look like. I felt no reason to explain the changes in her parents' house. Jack and I had thoroughly discussed them, and he seemed excited about the new look of our home.

Carol was a younger version of Mabel with her brown hair and blue eyes. When she attended our wedding, she seemed nice enough, but I remember overhearing her whispering to the neighbors that her poor mother had only been gone eighteen months before Jack and I married. Perhaps she was jealous or upset that there was another woman in her mother's house. Some of her conversation left me feeling defensive, and I had to keep reminding myself to be as nice to Jack's children as he was to mine.

It was a relief when Carol and her children left four days later. I couldn't help saying to Jack shortly afterward as I was cleaning up, "You do realize that Emily would have been happy to have you over for meals. Carol didn't need to come here."

"I know that, Becky." He sighed. "I didn't ask her to come. Maybe she just wanted to spend a little time with her father. Even though she and her family have visited once a year since we've been out here, we've missed so much time together over the past eleven years. I enjoyed spending time with her and the boys."

"I understand how hard it is being away from your family. It's like a piece of you is missing. I apologize if I seemed rude in any way to her."

"I think you handled it well. I apologize to you for Carol's sharp tongue, and for your boys feeling like they needed to bunk down over at Emily's," he said as he took me into his arms. "Some of her comments were inappropriate and I'm sad to say, designed to make you feel uncomfortable."

I kissed his cheek. "Thank you for being you, Jack. I am very fortunate to be your wife."

***

In November that year, Emily gave birth to her second child, Thomas John Elwood. All the men were thrilled. Em and I were over the moon as well.

CHAPTER 14

I loved the role of a preacher's wife. Church activities brought people together, so I had many opportunities to interact socially with homesteaders in the area. It was a welcome relief from the isolation I had often felt as John's wife living on the cattle ranch.

On the other hand, politics often intruded into church matters. A few years later in 1887, Jack was under pressure from other preachers in the area to join the Prohibition Party to push its agenda. It surprised me that Jack was reluctant to join, and he seemed to avoid the issue as much as he could. He believed that, just like guns, the problem was not the liquor, but how it was abused by some who used it. I agreed with his logic, but my experience with men who drank excessively pushed me in the other direction. Jack begrudgingly reneged when Prohibitionists torched our fence late one night.

***

The bubble burst on my happy life the following year when Jack received a letter from the Council of Bishops. I could tell by the look on his face it was a serious matter.

"Oh, my goodness, Becky." He continued to stare at the letter. "I don't know how to tell you this."

"What, Jack? Just say it."

"A new minister is replacing me, and I'm being transferred to San Francisco."

Thoughts raced through my mind for a full minute before I said, "I can't move to San Francisco. My boys, my daughter, and my grandchildren are all here. Em needs help with the children, Matty's getting ready for college, and Josiah is still so unsettled—a loose cannon even, at times."

"I understand, Becky. I don't want to go either."

"Destroying peoples' lives doesn't seem very Christian to me."

"I wonder if they got wind of my lack of participation in the Prohibition Party and decided to ship me out of Texas?"

"Jack, I don't care. What are we going to do?"

"It's not for two months. I'll see what I can find out."

Jack's attempts were futile, and about a month later I started to pack. We had decided that I would move with him and every three months I'd return for a month to visit my children.

I had been feeling poorly and thought I was tired from packing. Nonetheless, I decided it might be a good idea to visit Dr. Abrams in town before we left. He examined me and then sat down in his chair.

"If I were you, Rebecca, I'd get my affairs in order. Your heart's not doing well."

"What—what are you saying?"

"I'm so sorry to have to tell you this, Rebecca. Your heart's weak and irregular. I'll give you some pills to help, but—"

I gasped, and Doc grabbed me by the arm. I heard myself saying, "On no. How long do I have?"

"Impossible to tell. But it's only a matter of time. In the meantime, you need to rest for a couple hours every day and avoid any physical or emotional distress. Has something been weighing on your mind?"

"That's kind of like closing the barn door after the horse is loose, don't you think?"

"I didn't mean it that way. It could help your condition now if you don't keep things to yourself as much. I know you well enough, Becky, to say you're a strong, proud woman. I just want you to know it's okay not to be sometimes."

I went home and thought about what he'd said, but I still couldn't bring myself to tell Jack or Em. The plans were made, and somehow, I managed to finish the packing. Emily and Tom looked forward to moving into our house which gave them more space for the children. I was leaving her in charge of Matty and Josiah—a tall order, but one that she graciously accepted.

We'd planned to take the train out on the Southern Pacific Railroad the following morning. That night I passed out onto the kitchen floor. Jack had gone over to Tom's for a short time. The next thing I remembered was the sound of Jack's voice as I awoke to him sitting on the floor with my head in his lap.

"My God, Becky. Are you all right?"

"I'm—I'm not, Jack," I said as I began to sob. The last few weeks of angst poured out of me. Jack cradled me in his arms for a while and then helped me up and over to the sofa.

"Let me send Tom to get Dr. Abrams. I think—"

"No, I have pills—over there in my bag."

Jack looked at me suspiciously as he handed them to me. "Please, Becky, tell me what's wrong."

"I didn't know how to tell you, or Em. I thought I'd take the pills, and everything would be all right."

Jack took my hand and kissed it. "Please, Sweetheart, I need to know."

"Dr. Abrams said I have a heart problem. It's weak and irregular—Jack, I will die sooner than either of us expected."

He looked like I'd hit him in the head with a log from the woodshed. "I can tell you one thing—we're not leaving here tomorrow. I'm not taking you away from your children."

"But what about your job? You could go and I'll join you later."

"I'm not leaving you, Becky. Don't you realize I love you more than I've ever loved anyone? Do you really think I would leave you here and let go of whatever precious time we have left together?"

"I wanted to be a good wife to you. I fear I've fallen short already."

"No, no, don't ever say that!"

Jack slept with his arms around me that night. In the days and weeks to come, I slowly regained my energy and rested daily as prescribed. Not going to San Francisco was a good decision for both of us. Shortly afterward, Jack learned that in view of the circumstances, he could remain pastor at the church. It touched me deeply to know that he would have stayed even if they fired him. He reassured me that he would have done whatever it took to take care of us.

CHAPTER 15

Surprisingly, two years later, my health appeared stable, and I was happily preparing for a wedding. Twenty-four-year-old Josiah planned to marry thirty-year-old Ellen, a widow with a young child. They had kept company for eighteen months, and I felt sure it was a good decision for him. His relationship with this older woman had calmed his restless ways, and he seemed to slide easily into the role of fatherhood.

The wedding was on a cool, windy day a week before Christmas. Matty came home from Baylor University where he was in his second year of pre-law studies, to stand as his brother's best man. Jack performed a lovely ceremony. While we were greeting the guests in the rear of the church, I fainted. Jack carried me into his office and stayed with me until I came around. I opened my eyes to Em first, crying tears onto my dress. She suddenly stopped when she saw I was awake.

"Mama, where's your pills?"

"I'm not sure—if they aren't in my coat pocket, then they are home on the kitchen counter."

"They aren't in your coat. I'll send Tom to fetch them."

"Let me take her home, Em," Jack said. "If she's feeling better later, we'll come by for the reception."

Despite my protests, Jack carried me to the carriage and drove us home. I reassured everyone on the way out that I was fine and to please continue into the church hall for the reception. Matty and Josiah came to the house shortly after we returned. I told them to lose their concerned faces and get back to the reception. It irritated me to think I was casting a shadow over such a happy occasion. I felt better later, but we never returned to the church hall. I wanted to avoid the curious looks and any questions my fainting episode may have propagated. Guess I was like my mother in that respect.

Speaking of Mother, she passed away two weeks later. Even with the trains all the way through now, I knew I couldn't make the trip. Em wanted to go but was eight months pregnant. The last thing she needed was all that bouncing around. I only hoped that the family left there would understand.

Josiah and Ellen came to me the following day. "Mama, we want to go to the funeral for you. There should be someone there from our family," said Josiah.

"We want to help you, Mrs. Elwood—I mean Becky," said Ellen. "In fact, it could be partly a honeymoon. My parents would look after Henry."

It sounded like a reasonable solution, so I agreed. The next day, Matty took me to a lawyer about power of attorney papers for Josiah in case he needed to sign papers on my behalf.

"Ma, let me take this semester off from school. I'd like to spend more time with you."

"No, Matty, you belong in school. Your life now should be more about your future than your past."

"Without my past, I wouldn't be where I am today. I want you to know I'm grateful for all you and Pa did for me. I feel bad for saying this—but the best thing you ever did was to take me away from him for that year. I felt better about myself after that. Even though I loved Pa, I knew after that, it was only you, Em, and my brothers who really cared about what was best for me." After a short pause, he continued as his voiced cracked, "Especially you, Ma. I don't know what I'm going to do without you."

His words shot right to my heart, and my silent tears washed away a bit of the guilt that still lingered there. "You'll put one foot in front of the other and keep moving ahead as you always have. I'm so proud of the man you've become, Matty. A part of me will always be with you, cheering you on, I promise."

Two days later, Josiah and Ellen boarded the train in Dallas.

***

The impact of Mother's death hadn't hit me. I hadn't even cried. Could it be that I was becoming comfortable with the concept of death? In some ways, it had become a companion to me. Thoughts of it haunted me daily. A few days later, I breeched the subject with Jack.

"Where do we go when we die, Jack?"

"I wish I could describe it to you, Becky. I know it's a good place—full of love where you will reunite with your loved ones. I wouldn't expect any less from God, who literally defines love. He's not the vengeful God the Bible often implies."

"Jack, don't you believe in the Bible? You preach from it all the time."

"Indeed, I believe in much of it as a guide for living, but God speaks to us much louder through the heart, not the written word. Sweetheart, don't doubt that God has stood by you in times of need. Surely you have felt his love and strength."

"I think I do sometimes, but then I wonder why this is happening to me. I think maybe it's a punishment or something, and then I get mad at God—I mean I've tried to live a good life and do the right things. Perhaps it's because I didn't visit my parents enough, or I left John, or I didn't go to church—"

"None of that is true. I'll let you in on a little secret. I was mad at God when I first found out about your heart condition. How could I lose the love of my life after only a few years of marriage? Even though I'm a preacher, I still react in ordinary ways in my personal life."

"It must have been difficult for you to be mad at God and preach his word every week."

"It was, for about two weeks. During that time, God helped me to understand emotionally what I knew intellectually—that death is not a punishment, but rather a natural transition from life. We don't understand many of God's plans, but it doesn't mean there isn't a higher purpose. Now I'm truly grateful for each day we wake up together, even more than before."

"I'm so fortunate, Jack, to have you in my life. I want you to understand how much of a comfort you've become to me and to my children, as well. I appreciate every minute you've spent with them, reassuring them and overall being an excellent father. You listen to them—that's something they didn't get from John. He always seemed to brush them off or get mad. They think the world of you and Tom."

"I love your children, Becky, as if they are my own."

"That puts my mind at ease," I said as I put my arms around him and lay my head on his shoulder.

***

Josiah and Ellen returned a month later. Josiah dropped Ellen off at home and came right over to see me.

He leaned down and kissed my forehead. "You look good, Ma. How have you been feelin'?"

"Pretty good, most of the time. I'm taking a new pill now, and it seems to work better." I was pleased to see that getting married and traveling across the country had matured and polished him off a bit.

"How did it go in Philadelphia?"

"At times it was sad, but I was so excited to meet the family—all those aunts, uncles, and cousins I barely knew I had. Here's the jewelry you wanted. The stuff from the house should be here in a few days."

I began to sort through Mother's jewelry. "Mom, I wanted it to be a surprise, but I can't wait to tell you. We found your cradle in the attic. Aunt Betty said you slept in it, so I packed it with the other stuff that's being shipped."

"I'd totally forgotten about that, Josiah. Oh, I'm so happy!" I knew Em would want to use it. "Now all my future grandchildren can sleep in it."

"The finish on it's dull, but Tom and I will make it look nice and sturdy."

"I know it'll look beautiful for the new little one."

"Mama, Grandma left you everything except for some pieces of furniture she gave to her sisters. I put the house up for sale, and the agent will telegraph you when it sells. Also, here's a check to you from the bank."

I glanced at the check. The sum was more than I expected, and I looked forward to sharing it with all the children. I felt comfortable that with the money

John had left and the proceeds from this estate, all my children and grandchildren would have a good start in life.

"Thank you, Josiah, so much for taking care of this for me, for all of us. I don't know what I would have done without you." I reached out my arms to my son, and he leaned over for a long hug. He didn't pull away first as he usually did and must have sensed how I loved him more now than I ever had before.

A week later, little Emily Rebecca was born. And yes, she slept in her cradle the first night.

CHAPTER 16

I'd been feeling stronger, and it shocked me when Doc Abrams said that my heart was doing poorly, worse than two months ago.

"I'm so sorry, Becky, but quite frankly I'm not sure how you've survived this long."

"Must be God's will," I quipped.

I'd been having quite a few conversations with God lately. Relaxing into the notion of dying had begun to feel more comfortable. I was at peace with leaving, but not with the effect it would have on my family.

"Will I still love you after I die, Jack?" I asked as we lay in bed that night.

"Yes, I certainly hope so, Angel. I believe that love is timeless. God loves us eternally."

Tears welled up. "I don't want to leave you alone, Jack, I love you more now than the day we married. You've been so good to me. From you, I've learned the true meaning of unconditional love."

"It's the best kind of love. When you love someone without expectation, you can never be disappointed." He smiled. "However, I have to admit I'd be somewhat disappointed if you didn't love me a bit more personally as well." Jack turned on his side toward me and put his arm around my waist. "Don't think for one minute that I won't love and think about you every day of my life left on Earth. Our life together means the world to me. Why, you've brought so much warmth and joy into my world. You've accepted me and allowed me to be who I am," he said. "I never experienced that until I found you."

"I can say the same about you, Jack. These last few years have been some of the best of my life. Despite everything that's happened, I feel a peace and contentment with you I've never known before. Your love has changed me, and I've gotten to know God better, all because of you."

We settled into each other's arms until I heard Jack breathing with a light snore. I rolled away from him as my thoughts flashed back to the people in my life and decisions I'd made.

I had no doubt I was meant to move to Texas. My childhood longings led me here for many reasons—reasons I could never have imagined as my life bloomed into so much more beyond the desire to marry a cowboy. I just hope I didn't make it too hard for my parents. I know they didn't like being away from me, but they loved me enough to bring me to Texas. I will be forever grateful to them for that.

I was at peace about my relationship with Papa. He understood me in a way Mother never could, and I looked up to him many times as my guiding light. I was a little sad that Mother and I never experienced the same strong connection—it seemed we never totally understood each other. I did the best I could, but there were times I knew I didn't live up to her expectations.

John sparked a fire in my body and soul. He was the love of my life and gave me four wonderful children. I learned how hard life could be living as a rancher's wife and being married to a man who could not love me the way I had hoped. He wasn't a bad man, just carried too many wounds from childhood that had scarred his soul a bit. There was a dark side to him that cast a shadow over the way he looked at life. Sadly, he and I never saw the world in quite the same way.

After Emily left, I began feeling like I would die if I stayed with John. That's why I had to put myself first at that point and leave. It was then I began to trust that my heart would never lead me astray. It's strange how the heart can take the reins from you but still allows you to think you're in control.

My children had always been the most important thing to me. It was difficult to let go of the guilt I felt about leaving Owen and Josiah when Matty and I moved to Philadelphia. It helped when I came to realize that God has a plan for all of us and that my leaving was part of it, both then and now. Had I been able forgive John for causing Owen's death? I was still working on it, but I was almost there.

My thoughts turned to Jack—sometimes, we really do save the best for last now, don't we?

***

Two months later, the weather turned nice, and the children needed some new clothes. Despite the doc's prognostications, I was still feeling well, and Em suggested we go into town. We left baby Emily with Ellen and went shopping with Henrietta and Tommy. Right after we crossed a street, Tommy realized he had dropped his little stuffed horse and yanked his hand away from mine as he ran back into the street to get it.

"Tommy, no!" I screamed as I ran after him. I shoved him out of the way of the carriage that was barreling down upon us. I tripped and felt the pain of the horse's hooves treading across my lower back. The carriage wheels soon crushed my neck.

***

At the age of fifty-six, I left the world of my dear loved ones. My heart must be part of my soul because I still feel my love for my family. You were right, Jack. Love really is eternal.

About the Author

SHIRLEY SORBELLO is an inspirational writer of fiction and non-fiction. "Where the Heart Goes" is her debut novella. "That's Just the Way It Is," released in September 2013, was her first self-published short story. This was followed by a stand-alone sequel entitled "Return to Texas" in March 2014. The following year, Shirley edited and published "Martha's Words," a book of her grandmother's poetry written around 1900. Her writings tend to reflect her background in psychology and her spiritual perspective on life.

Writing about the Old West was not too much of a stretch for her. Shirley is part of the generation who grew up in the 1950s, when watching the latest western on TV was an everyday occurrence. She recalls traveling as a child through the southwestern states, especially Texas, numerous times with her parents often on the way to Mexico. She finds that the culture of the West in the 1800s brings her a sense of comfort.

For almost thirty years, Shirley was employed in the human services field as a social worker, therapist, and administrator. A few years ago, she retired into the world of writing, something she had always wanted to pursue. In addition to writing, Shirley enjoys spending time with family and friends, music, traveling, genealogy, photography, and chocolate.

Ms. Sorbello is a native of southern New Jersey. She majored in psychology at Rutgers University and later attended Widener University where she graduated with a master's in social work in 1995.

At the present time she is working on a novel with a reincarnation theme entitled "Trip to a Lifetime" as well as a non-fiction book about soulmates.

CONNECT WITH SHIRLEY SORBELLO

WEBSITE
www.shirleysorbello.com
EMAIL
spsorbello@gmail.com
FACEBOOK
https://www.facebook.com/ShirleySorbelloAuthor
INSTAGRAM
www.instagram.com/shirleysorbello

Made in the USA
Middletown, DE
10 November 2021